An Erotic Interracial Romance

Bundles

Hunter Briggs

Published by Hunter Briggs, 2024.

AN EROTIC INTERRACIAL ROMANCE

First edition. September 23, 2024.

ISBN: 979-8227451460

Written by Hunter Briggs.

Table of Contents

Going for Gold

Chapter 1

Mie wore her silver medal in a white, overflowing dress as she ate ice cream from a cone in the Olympic Village.

She had a faint smile on her face, but her mind was fixated on the previous ping-pong final, where she had narrowly lost to a more refined, experienced player from her home country, China.

Mie stopped suddenly at the sidewalk and watched a gaggle of ladies giggling as they walked past her.

She was slightly amused by the look on their faces, but this moment made Mie realize that she was incredibly bored. She took a long look at the ice cream and traveled up in a reverie to the moment she lost the final.

Mie was stuck in that moment, enacting strategies that would have put her in a better position to win. Her face brightened, accommodating a cheerful smile.

"I have never seen anyone look at a cone of ice cream that way."

Mie was startled by the sound of this voice. She straightened her face and found a tall, broad-shouldered, dark-skinned man.

Mie took a step back, surprised by the size of the man before her. He was almost twice her height.

Mie took another step backward, intimidated by his height, until she took a firmer look at his face. He had dark facial stubble and long dreadlock black hair, and his constricted hazel eyes were peaceful and calm.

"Did I take you by surprise?" He asked, taking a step forward and closing the distance between them.

Mie's brown eyes were fixed on his lips and handsome visage. Quickly, she lost the look of concealed fright that initially struck her face.

"No. Yes. Not really," she responded and quickly smiled, taking a deep breath. Her English was broken as it was her second language to her.

She dropped her eyes on his black sweats and quickly examined his ridged shape, before taking a quick glance at his black sneakers, hoping he didn't catch her gawking at him.

"Are you fine?" He asked, concernedly.

Mie nodded affirmatively. Her eyes were fixed on his white, tight shirt. She didn't know what was coming of her. Since she's been at the village, she'd seemed captured by the African men. Their dark skin and muscles were like nothing she'd seen in her home country.

"Are you sure?" He asked.

"Yeah. I am just overthinking some stuff," Mie replied.

"I see? You think you should have gotten gold, don't you?" He asked, his eyes fixed on Mie's silver medal as it slightly dangled underneath her perky breasts.

"I don't want to think about it, but you tend to wonder what could have been," Mie responded.

"I think you already have the mindset of a champion. You have a great future ahead of you."

"You don't know me," Mie responded.

"Yeah. Just as I didn't know you speak English. But faith can lead us down the right path."

"So you have faith in a stranger, huh?" Mie asked, stroking her long, dark hair.

"Lots of great things have happened because two strangers met."

Mie was impressed and took a quick look at his piercing, studious eyes. She took her eyes from his face quickly, unable to deal with the sexiness that oozed out of his inky eyes.

"What's your name?" He asked.

"Mie."

"Well, Mie. I am Jordan."

"Jordan. Are you a basketballer?" Mie asked.

"Nah. I am a heavyweight boxer."

"Hmm. Interesting. From the US?"

"Yeah. Why is your English so good?" Jordan asked.

"I studied English in China."

"Nice, I always wanted to learn Mandarin."

"You have interest in China?"

"Of course. I love your country. Everything is beautiful there. Including it's people."

Mie smiled and stared deeply into Jordan's eyes, wondering what captured her in those few moments with him.

"Your ice cream is melting," Jordan said, smiling wildly.

Mie shook her head and started eating her ice cream while taking frequent looks at Jordan's face.

"Are you a great boxer?" Mie asked.

Jordan smiled, nodding.

"I think I'm pretty good. I'm going for gold. I just got into the semifinals."

"Congratulations."

"Want to take a stroll with me?" Jordan asked.

"Of course."

Mie was smiling as she stretched her hand towards him. Jordan wrapped his big, brawny hand around hers and pulled her close as they walked across the sidewalk.

Although Mie felt incredibly small beside him, she felt safe and loved his taut arms and body.

While she licked her ice cream, she kept thinking about touching his stomach. She wanted to see whether it was as taut as his arms. She was also curious about other things as her eyes drifted towards the waistband of his sweats. She had heard of African men have larger members and was curious if Jordan was bigger too.

Silence prevailed between them as they walked together. The orange glow of sunset faded away imperceptibly, ushering in a gray ambiance that presaged night.

"Have you had fun so far?" Jordan asked, breaking the moment of silence between them.

"Fun? No. To be honest, I feel lonely. Maybe it's because I'm introverted. My roommate doesn't even stay in the room. She prefers to spend time with other people."

"That's not your fault," Jordan responded, seriously.

"I know. But sometimes I feel I'm not so attractive. Maybe that's why..."

"Don't say that about yourself," Jordan cut in, interrupting her. "You are beautiful. And you have a gorgeous smile. I don't think I've seen a more beautiful smile in my life."

"You are just flattering me," Mie responded.

"No. I watched you for some time before I came close. I felt something. The smile I saw on your face is the kind I want to wake up to every day," Jordan said, stopping and staring deep into her eyes.

Mie exuded a blushed smile that made her eyes really small as she looked up at him.

"That's the smile I'm talking about," Jordan said, intensifying the smile on her face.

Mie descended into a spell of shaking her head as she smiled. She dropped her face and started nodding.

Jordan was patient with her. He had a smile on his face as he gently caressed the back of her hand with his thumb.

"God. My cheeks hurt," Mie said, raising her face up. She looked into his eyes, retaining the smile on her face.

Gradually, Mie stopped smiling as she locked eyes with him. There was a remarkable silence in her eyes that opened room to intense imaginations. She thought about kissing him and having the full weight of his body against her.

"Sorry," Mie said, shaking her head.

"About what?" Jordan asked.

"It's just..."

"You can tell me..."

She pulled her hand away from his grip and touched his stomach before dropping the ice cream trash in her other hand in a trash can on the sidewalk.

She took his hand, unable to wrap her hand across his wrist.

"Do you want to sit?" she asked.

"Yeah."

Holding hands, they continued forward, edging closer to the dormitories.

Mie stopped at the side of an empty wooden bench that overlooked the dormitories. She sat down and tapped the space beside her, beckoning Jordan to sit.

"I feel really lively around you," Mie said.

"I was thinking the same thing."

"It is crazy, but I haven't really felt this way around anyone in this village," Mie said thoughtfully. She started tapping the edge of her lips trying to think of the right words to translate her feelings to Jordan.

"Energy can be intoxicating at times, you know. I was just thinking that I would be a lot more inspired if you watched my semifinal bout," Jordan responded.

"Really?"

"Yeah."

Mie stretched her hand forward, touching his stomach and taking a deep breath as soon as she felt it.

She adjusted her hand to his chest, feeling his heartbeat.

"You have a really strong body," she said, in a hushed tone.

The grayness of the day was slowly swallowed by the engulfing rays of darkness. The streetlights at the sidewalks and around the dormitories provided measured patches of illumination across the Olympic village.

Mie drew closer to Jordan, wiping off the distance between them. She dropped her head on his shoulder.

"Do you ever think of the future?" She asked.

"I like to take each day as they come. I think it makes me really open to the gifts of life."

"You have a great philosophy," Mie responded.

"What about you?" Jordan asked.

"I don't really want to think about it. But sometimes I feel that the future would be really lonely for me," Mie responded.

"Not with that smile," Jordan shot back quickly. "You have a smile that the world cannot afford to ignore."

"I wish I could hear that more often," Mie responded.

Jordan placed his hands on the sides of her face and stared intently at her.

"You are special. And sometimes special people get lonely and question..."

Mie left a kiss on his lips, shutting him up. Jordan's eyes dilated slightly as he looked back at her. Her face was inches away from his, and amorous plumes sifted out of her eyes.

Jordan opened his mouth to say something, but nothing came out. His expression conveyed confusion and deep desire. His eyes searched her face and eyes like torchlights in a forest.

"Do you want to see my dorm?" She asked, taking his hand and standing up.

Jordan opened his mouth again, but he closed it back quickly.

He stood up without offering a response to her question. Instead, he followed her, tackling the rush of fluids in his stomach. Desire ran up his spine, leaving a rash of gooseflesh on his arms.

Mie kept her face forward, walking quickly, and ignoring the faces on her way. She knew what she was doing was wrong. The Chinese had strict rules about men being in the female dormitories. Even worse, Jordan was American. If anyone told her coaches she would be in big trouble. However, at that moment, she didn't care. She was done overthinking things. She knew it was time to act and, in that moment, she wanted Jordan.

Jordan looked like a child. A big baby led by a small mother. He was star-stuck being led by Mia down the hallway. He knew he should be focusing on his fight, but in that moment all he could focus on was Mie. It was hard not to see her ass shake as she stomped through the crowd. The jiggle of her body with every step. It was intoxicating. Like a drug he couldn't get enough of.

He dropped his face as movements started in his crotch area. His sweats rose in his center, impelling him to place one hand across his body, hiding his erection.

Mie opened a door and walked inside with him. She closed the door and looked into his eyes.

There was something about this version of Mie that Jordan didn't see outside the dormitories. She looked like a cat—small, quiet, but calculative and brave.

The intensity of her stare gave off her intent, like writings on a piece of paper. She leaned against the door, watching him as he stood two yards away.

Silence prevailed, but their minds were busy. Questions were asked. Desires were ignited.

Jordan's cock bulged forward, but he was unwilling to cover his erection this time.

She dropped her eyes on his sweats and succumbed to a deep exhalation.

Keeping her eyes on his cock, Mie pulled away from the door. Her stride was slow, but her gaze was ferocious. She regarded him like a meal—a healthy, palatable meal prepared with the blessings of God.

His sweats continued to tilt forward as if there was no limitation to the size of his erection.

When Mie drew close to him, she looked up at his face. His eyes were constricted, and Jordan yearned for her touch.

Mie placed her hand on his chest and gently caressed him. Jordan took a deep breath as she slid her hand down to his navel. Mie fondled it slightly before dipping her hand past his waistband.

Mie instantly realized the strength of his erection. Jordan's dick had broken through his underwear, leaving a gaping hole at the center.

His dick was eight inches long and had several long, pulsing veins.

Mie felt his dick and shivered slightly as it pulsed in her grip.

"So big and fat," she said, in a faint tone.

Mie couldn't wrap her hand across his dick, which continued to pulse as it grew harder, becoming as strong as metal.

"I never thought an African man would be so big..." She whispered, softly.

Jordan was quiet, but beads of sweat formed on his brow as he watched her. She ran her hands across his length as she looked up at him, gauging his expression.

His breathing was heavy, and from the look in his eyes, it was easy to see that he was thinking about all the bad things he wanted to do with her.

Holding tightly to his dick, Mie started walking towards him, forcing him to back away until he was standing at the side of her bed.

Mie pushed him with a forefinger, and Jordan landed heavily on his back as if he had been hit by a knockout punch.

Mie's eyes were barely open as she jumped onto him, kneeling between his legs and dropping her face on his dick as it extended upward.

She caressed his cock with her face cheeks and looked towards his face. Her eyes never leaving his as she sensually teased him.

"I want to do crazy things with you, mister heavyweight," she said, and dipped the fat tip of his dick into her mouth.

Mie needed to open her mouth as wide as possible to fit his dick inside. She was impervious to the pain on her cheeks as she kept taking more of his dick in her mouth.

When Jordan's dick was halfway in her mouth, Mie's eyes bulged, and she gurgled, obviously struggling to deal with his fat, pulsing, big dick, but she continued to keep his black dick in her mouth, embracing the pain and struggle.

Blobs of saliva trickled down from the corners of her lips as she kept his dick firmly in her mouth.

Jordan gritted his teeth as he watched her.

In a sudden rush of madness, Mie started moving her face up and down, rolling her tongue at the tip of his black dick.

His legs trembled from the movement of her tongue at the tip of his dick, but Mie was barely observant of his responses. She sucked hard on his cock, breathing heavily.

Moments later, she pulled his dick from her mouth and went for his balls. Mie sucked in his scrotal sac, sucking hard on his balls as she moved her hand up and down his dick.

Jordan tightened his thighs, pulling his upper body up slightly.

"Fuck," he said, biting hard on his lower lip.

His dick grew harder in her grip, and the head of his dick became redder and pulsed intensely.

Mie was still sucking hard on his balls when he pulled away from her and grabbed her. He took a deep breath, his eyes constricting.

"My turn," he said, lifting her from the bed easily. He dropped her in the position he had taken when she sucked his dick.

Jordan furled her dress up to her face, wasting no time in getting into the business matter.

Jordan grabbed her black G-string panties and tore them off her waist. He wiggled his tongue in the gusset of her underwear before turning towards her.

As Jordan rolled his tongue across his lips, Mie realized that Jordan had the longest tongue she had ever seen.

He dropped his face on her crotch, placing his hands on her thighs.

Jordan started rolling his tongue on Mie's brown clit, which was already swollen and pulsed softly.

"Jeez. Fuck," she moaned lightly, trembling as Jordan intensified the movement of his tongue on her clit.

Her brown clit grew even bigger as he wiggled his tongue intensely on it. Slowly, he took his tongue to her pussy and dipped the full length of his tongue in her pussy.

Mie grabbed a pillow and threw it away from the bed, biting hard on her lower lip.

"This is so good. God. God. Yeah. Oh. Yeah. Oh shit. Yes. That's it. That's fucking it," Mie cried.

Her eyes gleamed, and her face was sweaty.

Mie's pussy throbbed as Jordan took his tongue to the top of her pussy, fluttering it. Her pussy juice thickened and trickled down into his mouth, but Jordan continued to keep his tongue deeply submerged in her pussy.

Mie grabbed the sheets, pulling them.

"Oh! My God. What's this? Shit. Oh my God. Yes. Yes. Oh shit. Oh shit."

She drew closer to him as if she wanted his whole head in her pussy.

Jordan could feel the tremble in her thighs. He could sense the increase in her vaginal secretion as it pulsed relentlessly.

"Oh. Please. I need your dick. Get it inside me. Fuck my pussy," she moaned.

Instead of giving Mie his dick, Jordan decided to dip his large middle finger in her pussy.

Mie dropped her face on the bed and bit hard on the sheet as soon as he started fingering her. Her pussy tightened against his fat finger, and she wiggled her toes as he fingered her.

He had his eyes on her, maintaining his intensity and luxuriating in the impact of his finger.

"God! Something is happening... Damn... damn! God, oh God."

Mie's breathing came in snatches as an eerie vibration engulfed her body. She looked like she was licking close to passing out.

Jordan kept fingering her pussy, showing no mercy as Mie's eyes suddenly became white.

"Yeah. Oh! Oh! Yes. Yes."

Blobs of thick, slimy fluids shot out of her pussy, flying two meters upward and landing on her crotch.

Jordan suddenly dropped his face on her pussy as she started squirting. He pressed his tongue against her peehole and wiggled it, applying pleasurable pressure as she squirted.

Mie's eyes were still egg-white. She squeezed her hands, falling back down on the bed as she struggled to contain the pleasure that afflicted her.

Jordan raised his face up and unzipped her dress, throwing it on the floor. Also, he took off her medal.

Her breasts were firm and small, and her brown nipples were meaty and erect. Her skin was beige and flawless. She was perfect.

He fondled her nipple and wiggled his tongue on it.

"Oh! My God. You are going to kill me with pleasure. You are fucking going to kill me with pleasure," she cried.

He pushed her legs apart, barely fitting in the space between them.

He grabbed his dick, which was hard and looked like a rock.

Mie watched the pulsing veins on his dick. She trembled at the pre-cum-leaking-black-monster about to enter inside her.

As Jordan pressed the head of his dick in her pussy, he encountered a bit of difficulty getting his dick inside because his dickhead was too fat and Mie's pussy was tiny.

Mie tried to spread her legs apart to give him more room to penetrate her, but Jordan leaned towards her, covering her entire body as he lay on her.

He kept one elbow on the bed to reduce the pressure of his weight on her body. In this position, Jordan pressed his dick hard against her pussy and penetrated her.

"God," she screamed, trembling as his dick went inside her. He was too big. A sweet painful pleasure swept through her and she felt like a virgin again.

Jordan pushed his dick inside her gradually. He could feel the walls of her pussy as they clenched hard against his fat, long, black dick. He gasped from the vice grip around him.

Once his dick was halfway in her pussy, Jordan made slow in and out movements inside her. Her pussy juice thickened as it expanded, accommodating the sheer size of his black dick.

Mie's mouth was agape, and her hands were clenched as he maintained his slow in and out movement.

Mie couldn't even see his face because she was so small as she lay flat below him.

Moments later, Jordan extended his dick inside her pussy, intensifying the tremble on her thighs.

As her pussy throbbed, Jordan kept taking his dick inside slowly until the full length of his dick was inside her pussy.

"Oh! My God. I can feel it in my stomach," she moaned, her lips quavering.

Her moans were followed by gentle thrusts as her pussy soaked his dick and created more room for intense thrusts.

Slowly, Jordan increased the pace of his thrusts, slacking the walls of her pussy as he fucked her.

"Yes, yes, yes. Take it. Take this fucking pussy. I love your African dick. Oh, it's so big. Oh fuck me. There's nothing like this You're a fucking champion. Yes. Yes. Fuck it hard. Own it. Own this fucking pussy. Yes. Fuck. Fuck," Mie moaned, tears trickling down from the corners of her eyes.

Jordan smiled and pounded her flesh hard with powerful thrusts.

Mie wailed, as she began to question everything in her life.

"Why are you so good? Why do you fuck me so well? God! I love your dick. I fucking love this. Yes. Yes. Fuck me. Yeah. Fuck my pussy hard," she begged, unclenching her hand and pulling the sheets from the edges of the bed.

Jordan increased the pace of his thrusts, taking the full-length of his dick in and out of her pussy continuously.

"Fuck. Fuck. I think I am going to come again. I am coming. Oh my God. You fucking, crazy heavyweight. You fuck my pussy so hard. Fuck. Yes. Fuck," she cried.

Jordan took a deep breath and picked Mie up from the bed. He stood with her as he kept his dick deep in her pussy.

Jordan moved from the bed and took her to the wall. Pressing her back against the wall and spreading her legs apart, Jordan fucked her hard.

Mie left painful bites on his arm, overwhelmed by the pleasure that engulfed her.

"You devil. Fuck. You're going to fuck me to death. You're going to kill me with your dick. Yes. Yes. Yes. Harder... right there... that's it. That's it. Yes. Yes. I'm coming. I'm fucking coming," she moaned, biting hard on her lip as a fresh rush of fluids shot out of her pussy.

Jordan continued to fuck her hard as she squirted.

Mie started whimpering as he maintained the intensity of his thrusts. White fluids started seeping out of her pussy and her eyes became egg-white again.

Mie became quiet, reaching a depth of pleasure where words eluded her.

Grabbing tightly to her body with his dick still fully submerged in her pussy, Jordan took her to the bed and slammed her against the bed, keeping his dick deep in her pussy.

The cardboard frames of the bed gave way, succumbing to their combined weight. The terrible landing seemed to take his dick deeper in her pussy.

"Is your dick is growing? Damn it. Shit. What kind of God made your dick? Fuck. This is so good," she moaned.

Jordan tilted his face up, breathing heavily and dilating his eyes.

"I am coming," he said in a throaty, husky voice.

He left quick, deep thrusts in her pussy and pulled his dick from her pussy.

As soon as he took his dick from her pussy, gobs of semen shot out of his dick, landing on her face and body. His legs trembled, and his dick continued to pulse as he held on to it.

After the intense escapade, Mie could barely move.

The bed was steeped to one side, and Jordan quickly worked on the cardboard frames below, straightening the bed while Mie was still lying on it.

Afterwards, he carried Mie to the bathroom and took a quick bath with her.

Jordan applied soap to Mie's body and bathed her while she leaned against the bathroom wall, her knees threatening to buckle under her.

Mie was feeling stronger when they returned to the bedroom. She changed into a fresh, red nightdress and watched as Jordan wore his clothes.

She sat in her bed, watching as Jordan stood at the foot of the bed, seemingly introspective.

"You want to leave now?" Mie asked.

"No. I want to talk to you," he replied.

"Then join me in bed," Mie requested.

Jordan joined her and placed his hand on her back as she rested her head on his shoulder.

"What's on your mind?" Mie asked

"I really enjoyed this so much," Jordan replied.

"You look really experienced. I haven't been fucked this way before," Mie said, raising her face up.

"I think I'm just strong. It can be misinterpreted for experience."

"Fair enough."

"Do you have a boyfriend?" Jordan asked.

"No. Do you have a girlfriend?" Mie asked.

"No. I broke up with my ex-girlfriend a month ago."

"That's quite early," Mie suggested.

"Yeah. I know. But it has been a long time coming," Jordan said, turning towards her. "I feel more alive with you, Mie. I can't explain it."

"Maybe it is just the lust. Maybe you'll feel different when it settles."

"I don't think so. I feel like I can start something incredible with you. I feel like this is the start of something beautiful," Jordan said seriously.

"I don't know. I feel..."

"Do you have someone else in mind?" He asked.

"No."

"Do you think I deserve a chance to be with you?" Jordan asked.

"I really want to be with you, but I don't want to be a distraction. I don't want you to make a relationship decision because of a great sex."

"No. That's not what this is about. Your smile was what drew me to you. I want you around me. I want you to watch my matches. Be at my side. I want you in my life," Jordan reiterated, placing one hand on her shoulder.

Mie was convicted by the tone of his voice. Jordan placed his hands on her shoulder and drew closer to her, pressing his lips against hers. He kissed her, sucking hard on her lower lip and fondling her hair gently.

Moments later, he drew apart from her and looked into her eyes.

"What do you say?" He asked.

"I will be by your side. To be honest, I was instantly attracted to you as soon as I saw your face," she whispered.

Jordan smiled and started another round of kissing with Mie.

Chapter 2

Jordan stood at the overhung altar of this sprawling Catholic Church, donning a black, creaseless suit. He was half-confined in his mind. His eyes were fixated on Mie's face as she walked down the aisle towards him. Her wedding gown was simple, her face was as beautiful as ever, and her smile punctuated the lovely poetry in his head.

A Harmonica of Somewhere Only We Know by Keane blared across the church, draining the congregation in a solemn, emotional mood.

Jordan's eyes gleaned with tears. His best man kept rolling a hanky across the corners of his eyes, wiping off his tears.

Mie was smiling and looked innocent in her wedding dress. Her father held her hand proudly, leading her to the altar.

As she drew closer to the altar and noticed the look in Jordan's eyes, her emotions were quickly translated to accommodate tears. It was easy to think about the intense beginning of their relationship. Perhaps it indicated that some things were meant to be.

Tears started rolling down from her eyes as she clambered up the stairs. She became increasingly drawn to the harmonica, embracing its intensity and lyrics.

Moments later, they stood apart from each other on the altar, separated by the width of the pulpit.

They barely listened to the preacher's message as they locked eyes, smiling as tears gathered in their eyes.

When they exchanged vows, most of the congregation were stricken by the emotion that tinged their voices. There was love in the air, and it was firmly expressed in the kisses that followed the exchange of vows.

In the reception, there was singing, dancing, dining, and unrestrained celebration.

Moments later, Jordan took the mic and stood at the side of the sprawling table where he sat with Mie.

He gave her a kiss and proceeded forward, facing the guests, who sat in chairs adjoined to round tables across the hall.

"Mie hasn't just been my lover. She has been so many things to me. From the first day I saw her smiling, I knew she would be important in my life. She became my muse and stayed by my side, rendering support as much as possible.

"Words cannot describe the inspiration I received from having her by my side. She made me even more focused. I wanted to win for myself, but I had another reason after I met her. I wanted her inspiration to be worth it.

"When I won gold at the Olympics, a lot of people talked about how I had worked hard for it and deserved it. They were right. Winning gold at the Olympics gave me a great platform to consolidate my career as a heavyweight boxer, but a lot of people didn't know how sad I was before I went to the Olympics, I didn't really see much value in life. I unleashed my anger on my opponents. I thought winning would make me feel better, but it didn't really make me feel better. Instead, it made me angrier. I always thought about damaging and destroying my next opponent. But when I found Mie, I found life. I found the desire to value this life and take my opportunities to love it as much as I can. And when I won gold in the Olympics, I didn't win it because I won the final of the heavyweight boxing. I won gold because I met Mie. She is gold. Going for gold has never felt so worthwhile," Jordan said, turning towards Mie, who had a hanky against her left eye.

"I love you so much, Mie. You are the breath of fresh air that I cannot stop taking. You are my answered prayer," Jordan said, tears gathering in his eyes.

A round of applause swept across the hall. Most of the guests stood up, clapping and cheering.

Mie left her chair and ran towards Jordan. She kissed his cheek and gave him a warm embrace, and from that kiss they lived happily ever after.

My Truth

Mary didn't know what to think as she followed her boyfriend into his apartment. She couldn't explain why she was so nervous. Her heart fluttered. She felt a cold chill down her spine, and her fingers felt like they were made out of pure electricity.

With every step, she felt like her insides were going to burst. Looking at her boyfriend, Malcom, she wondered if he too was feeling the same.

Malcom was black, and muscular. He played on the football team at the university, and they've been dating for about three weeks.

Honestly, if you asked her, Mary had no idea how a girl like her was dating a sexy hunk like Malcom. Physically she wasn't the ideal woman to be dating a college football player. Nerdy, pale, chubby, were adjectives to describe her. For a popular college football player like Malcom, he could have his pick of the litter of women. He could easy date a blonde model, yet he chose to be with a pear shaped, plus sized, geeky girl like her. Granted they both had the same interests in geek culture, but she always questioned why he was with her. What made her so special?

Sitting in the living room couch was Malcom's roommate. He was playing video games on the tv when they walked in. He gave Mary a smile and wave and then dapped up his roommate before resuming his game.

"Did you want check out my room?" He asked.

"Sure..." Mary breathed. She told herself to stay calm, but in reality she was freaking out. She didn't know what to expect. She'd never been invited to a boy's room. Not alone at least. She questioned if he expected to have sex with her.

While she was still a virgin, she wouldn't mind losing it with Malcom. For the time that she knew Malcom, he was a good man. Far better than any boyfriend that she had in the past. However, she didn't know his true intentions. Perhaps that's why he wanted her. He knew she was a virgin, and his end-goal was just to add another notch to his belt.

Following him to his room, she sat on the bed, and he sat next to her smiling.

"I really enjoyed the dinner and movie, Mary."

"So did I." She admitted.

"Watching that comic book movie really made me want to watch the first one. Did you want to watch it with me?"

"Are you sure?"

"Yeah, why? I thought you'd be down."

"I am, but when you invited me to your room, I thought you had other intentions..."

"Oh..." his eyes got wide as he read her mind. He rubbed the back of his head trying to find the right words to say.

"What?"

"Nothing it's just...I know you're a virgin, and I didn't want to rush you into anything you don't want."

"Really?"

"Yeah. Mary, I really like you."

"All of me? Even my plus size curves?"

He sighed and held her hands. His dreamy brown eyes peered deep into her own and he smiled, "Mary, I told you, all of that physical shit doesn't mean a thing. I like you for you. I find every inch of you sexy. I ain't like other guys. I like my women thick, and Mary you have all the curves in all the right places. I love your irresistible tits, your stunning thighs, and gorgeous smile. To me, you are prefect, and I wouldn't have it any other way."

Mary blushed and looked down at her feet.

"Hey..." he placed two fingers under her chin and brought her eye level with him. "I want you. I like you for you. Physical or not, you are the woman I want to be with."

"Really?"

"Oh course..."

She didn't question her feelings anymore as she jumped into his arms, kissing him. She didn't need to worry about nothing as she had her answer. She knew he liked her, like she liked him and that was enough. Her lips crashed into his as their kiss intensified.

"Malcom..." she breathed, feeling his hand explore every inch of her body.

"Yes, baby..." he gasped, licking her neck. Grasping at her clothes, bring her closer to him.

"I want you to be my first." She whispered, her body shuddering as she finally admitted her want.

His eyes opened wide as he took a moment to pause their love affair.

"Are you sure?"

"I've never been surer."

He grinned and kissed her once more. "I got a condom. I'll be right back. Get naked."

She nodded and hastily removed her clothes to lay underneath the covers. As she laid there, she watched as Malcom removed his own clothes and slip the rubber latex down his hard black shaft. Her insides quaked and her thighs became moist looking at his big black cock.

She breathed heavily wondering how such a larger member could fit inside her. He climbed into bed and kissed her once more. Laying on top of her he brushed a strand of her brown hair away from her face and smiled.

"Are you sure you want this?"

"I am. I am ready. I want you."

He grinned and kissed her once more before slipping inside her. Mary closed her eyes and gasped as a painful pleasure swept through her. Her toes curled and her legs naturally bent. It hurt at first, but the pain subsided and soon there was only pleasure.

Mary held onto Malcom's back as he pumped in and out of her. He groaned burying every inch he had inside her. Mary couldn't help but to moan. The magical feeling brought tears to her eyes as she shared the same love and passion that Malcom felt.

As he ground his body on top of her, Malcom arched his back to look into Mary's eyes. He smiled and kissed her pale lips.

"You feel amazing."

"I do?" She questioned, hoping that he felt the same pleasure she felt.

"Yeah, I am so happy that you're with me. This feels right. Doesn't it?"

"It does. I really does." She grinned.

"I love you." He admitted.

"What?" She gasped.

Malcom laughed and repeated himself. "I love you."

"You can't be serious; I mean we've been dating for three weeks; how can you know?"

"I just know. Trust me, I've been with other women, and nothing compares to you. You're funny, smart, beautiful. You get me on a level that no other woman does. No one compares to you. I can't explain this feeling. The easiest way to describe it is it's..."

"Love..." she cut him off.

"Exactly."

"I feel the same way. I love you too." She admitted.

He grinned and kissed her once more. After their tender and lingering kiss, he pressed his forehead against hers and whispered, "I'm going to finish in you, okay?"

"Yes, do it."

He grinned and pumped into her hard. Mary screamed as the friction was out of this world. She held him tightly and then felt him fill his condom with his seed. When he was done, he pulled out of her gasping for air.

"Damn that was amazing. How was your first time?"

"Amazing." She giggled. She cuddled his sweaty chest, and he held her tightly looking at the ceiling.

"Did you want to sleep over?" He asked.

"I wouldn't miss this for the world. Of course I'll stay over."

"Good. Give me a few minutes and we'd go again."

"Again?" she asked.

"If you think that first time was great, just wait for your second time."

"Oh, Malcom, I love you."

"I love you too, Mary."

The new couple kissed once more sharing their love for each other. Before tonight, Mary questioned what Malcom's true intentions was, but now she knew. She knew that he loved her and that she loved him. From then on, they lived happily ever after.

On the Beach

"I'm so happy that I'm married to you." My newlywed husband, Lamar grinned.

I smiled back at him as I laid on a towel outside on the beach. I could feel the warm sun on my pale curvy skin, while Lamar's dark muscular body glistened. I loved looking at his athletic form. We were an odd couple, as I was a bigger cubby woman and he had this Superman physique. At first glance you'd wonder why our pairing would happen, but both loved our physical features. He loved my plus sized curves, and I loved his muscles and big black cock. Call me a freak, but there's nothing like like taking a black man, and my new husband had it all. All twelve inches to be exact.

"Me too. I love this honeymoon." I ginned.

"I do too. This Caribbean island was such a great idea."

"Yeah, however I feel weird in this bikini."

"Why? You look sexy in it."

"I know *you* like it, but did you see everyone's look when I walked out in the lobby? They are probably wondering how a fat cow in a bikini like me could be with you."

"Babe, are you serious? We've been over this. I love every inch of you."

"Really?"

"Yes. You are my *woman*. I'm not ashamed."

"You're not?"

"Of course not. Any man would be lucky to have you."

"Yeah?"

"Yes, baby." He grinned, leaned closer to me, and kissed me. I groaned feeling his lips on me and his strong hands hold me.

"I love you." He whispered in between kisses.

"I love you too."

His hands grabbed the waist band of my bikini and I grabbed his hand.

"Babe what are you doing?"

"Proving to everyone that you're mine."

"But we're outside on a public beach."

"So? There's one one around."

"But someone could walk by."

"Let them watch. Let them see our love. Let them see how sexy you are when you take me dick. I want to take you right here on the beach with the same sun on my back and the sand in my toes. I want to hear you moaned with the sound of the waves crashing behind us. I want to feel your cum around my cock and see it drip all over the sand around us."

"Aww, baby."

"So what do you say?"

I gave him a naughty grin and pushed my bikini bottoms down.

He smiled back at me and began to finger me. I groaned feeling his finger glide in and out of me.

There was a thrill having sex on the beach. While no one was near, the thrill of knowing that someone could coming close made th sex better.

Lamar kissed me once more and pulled his finger away from my dripping pussy.

"Get on your knees."

I grinned and adjusted into doggy position. He slapped my ass and slipped inside me. He grunted hard, thrusting into me with vigor. I moaned, and my fingers dug into the sand. I loved feeling his hands grip my ass. He was a madman taking what wras his. Feeling very inch of him in the hot sticky sand was erotic and sexy. I didn't care that I was dirty I didn't care that my body was covered in sand. The sex was perfect. He was perfect.

We rolled in the sand and I was on top. He held my hips smiling as he watch me ride me.

"Yeah, take that dick."

"How does that feel?"

"Good. I love you."

"I love you too baby."

"Are you going... ah shit." I saw a couple walking towards us. And my husband and I both paused what we were doing as the couple walked by us and smiled. It was clear what was going on my husband's cock was out, I didn't have any bottoms. I was scared that we'd be called out for it or arrest, but the older couple didn't say anything. The man winked at me and they walked away towards the hotel room.

Once they were gone, Lamar and I both giggled.

"That was close." He breathed.

"It sure was."

"Let's finish this." He grinned.

"Yes. Fuck me hard baby."

"As you wish, baby."

We rolled in the sand once more, and he spread my legs wide. He grunted slamming to me, fucking me hard, pushing me deeper into the sand.

He smiled at me and said, "I love you."

"I love to too."

"You're beautiful, you know. Every inch of you. Every curve. You should be embarrassed of your size. I love your plus size."

"Aww baby."

"I fucking love you."

"I love you too." I repeated.

"Fuck, fuck, fuck...." He gasped and finished inside me. When he was done, he pulled of me, me watching as his cum leaked out of me onto the sand. He pulled up his shorts and I put my bottoms back one.

Another couple walked in the beach by us, but the damage had already been done. My husband had fucked me on the beach. He has sealed our new love and confirmed my doubts. I was right to marry this man. He was perfect for me, and I was perfect for him.

Mixed Doubles

Chapter 1

"Move to the left! The left! The..."

I didn't hear my coach as I collided into my mixed doubles teammate, Grace Chang. We both feel hard, and the yellow tennis ball bounced in-between us out of bounds.

"Ugh!" Our head coach rubbed his head in frustration and walked away.

Grace glared at me. "Stay out of my way."

"Your way? You were in mine!" I snapped back.

She rolled her eyes and got up from the green and blue hard tennis court. Her ass in her short white skirt shimmied as she stomped away from me towards her square of the court. She was mumbling something to herself in Chinese as she stood at the baseline readying herself for the next play. My teammate was Asian American, but I was beginning to understand that she cursed me out in mandarin instead of English.

She had an athletic frame, with toned legs and arms. She wore a white tank top and a short skirt. Sweat beaded her beige skin forehead as she leaned forward and swayed back and forth with her racket clutched by both hands. Her mind was focused on the next play as her eyes narrowed towards our mixed doubles sparring partners.

Bent over, I admired the curve of her ass. She would actually be cute if she wasn't such a bitch. Great tits, good ass, pretty smile, just a cunt. Sucked that all the beauty was wasted for her attitude.

I got placed with her because my other teammate sprained her ankle and was going to miss the US open tournament, and my coach thought it would be a good idea to team me up with a singles player who struggled to ever make it past the quarterfinals.

She was a good player, but a horrible doubles partner. She didn't let the game come to her, and she always wanted to be in control, which didn't help our play at all.

I stood up and glared at her. I dusted myself off and got into my ready position in the opposite square next to her.

"Y'all good?" Our coach asked.

"Yeah..." I snapped.

"Grace?" My coach asked.

"Yes, I'm fine." I grumbled at a low voice.

"Grace, if this isn't a good fit for you..." my coach began to say.

"I said, I'm fine!" She snapped, cutting my coach off.

He looked at me and shook his head. "Whatever. Let's start again." He looked towards our sparing mixed doubles partners and nodded giving them a head nod to start. The male lifted the ball and served it towards us.

"That's yours!" I yelled.

"I know..." she growled, slapping the shit out of the ball back towards the other teams. She gave me another angry glare before turning to face the other team. I could feel the toxic energy from her and I shook my head in frustration. I had no idea how I was going to work with her.

Chapter 2

I hated him. I hated every essence of him. His very presence annoyed me, but if I wanted to win, I had to work with him. Well, that is what my agent said. According to him, my sponsors were tired of me losing and were threatening to pull out if I didn't win an open. Thus, I'm stuck playing with Trevor Brown.

He's won an open before, but with a different partner, and when his female partner sprained her ankle, I thought I could be an easy replacement, however I now see it's the opposite.

He's stubborn, rude and wild. He doesn't play to the standards for doubles, instead he's a showboating asshole, preferring to do trick shots than to stick to the standards of play. He throws off my game and I fucking hate it. I hate him.

I mean look at him, I glared watching as he slapped the ball towards the other side. Trevor was wearing an athletic shirt and a pair of black shorts. His sweat drenched his dark toned arms and legs, as he moved with ease returning another serve. If he wasn't so annoying he could actually be cute, but his stubbornness was a major turn off.

The ball split between us once again and he rolled his eyes.

"Grace that was on your side!"

"No, it was yours. Call it out next time and perhaps I'd get to it."

"That's enough!" Our coach snapped.

"All you two is bicker. You are both good tennis players, but you can't work as a team. If you want to win, figure it out. Otherwise, just give up, you're not going to win the open. Take a few hours. Figure out what's going on and when you are ready to play as a team come and find me. Otherwise, I can't work with you both. You might as well drop out now." He shook his head and stomped away.

"Great, way to go asshole." I snapped.

"Yeah, this is totally *your* fault."

"My fault? Are you blind? If you actually knew anything about playing doubles, you'd know that you're in the wrong."

"I'm in the wrong! Seriously? I've actually won a major in tennis doubles. Have you? Oh yeah, you haven't. You haven't won shit. You're desperate. You're hoping to win something by jumping aboard my team. I'm your last hope before you lose everything."

I gasped and narrowed my brow at him.

"Yeah, that's right. I heard." He continued. "I'm your last hope. Without me, you are nothing."

I only saw red when I slapped him. He stood in shock holding his cheek. I didn't care anymore. I couldn't work with him. I refused to work with him. He was a monster, and I hated him.

Chapter 3

I felt like an asshole the moment she walked away. I pushed her too far. I was just frustrated. I wanted to win, and she was holding us back. Despite that I should have never said those things.

I walked into the women's locker room, trying to find her to apologize.

I found her getting her things together in her backpack. The moment she saw me her eyes opened wide.

"What in the hell are you doing here! It's the woman's locker room, prev."

"There's no one in here. Don't get your panties in a wad."

"Asshole." She continued to pack her things.

"I wanted to apologize to you." I admitted.

"No, need. I'm done."

"No, you're not. Stop bitching and let's get back out there."

"I'm not going to be your teammate. I can't work with you."

"So? You're good. We can figure it out."

"No, we can't. I'm done." She snapped.

I grabbed her hand and shook my head. "No, we're not. I'm not going to ask again."

"Take your hand off me." She snapped.

"Not until you come out with me."

"That's never going to happen. Take your hand off me!"

"Or what?" I smirked. She lifted her hand to slap me, but I caught it. "Not this time." I held both of her hands, and she struggled to break free from me.

She breathed deeply and her chest moved rapidly. My eyes lingered on her slim figure, and my eyes could stray from her firm breasts and flat stomach. I didn't know why, but my cock stiffened in that moment.

Her eyes peered into mine and call me crazy but in that moment, I wanted to kiss her. My eyes turned to her thin pink lips and my heart fluttered wondering what her lips would feel like in a kiss. My eyes lowered towards her perky tits in her tank top, and my fingers twitched wondering how soft and warm her breasts would be in my hands. I didn't know what was driving my lust, but my impure thoughts didn't end at her tits. Looking down at her skirt and tone beige skinned thighs, I wondered what her pussy would feel wrapped around my cock. I didn't want to think about having sex with her, but in the aggressive dominating position that I was in, the thought didn't leave. I didn't know what was coming over me, but there was something by sexy about the way she looked at me. I'd never felt this way about a woman before. How was it possible to hate someone yet physically want them?

Chapter 4

His lustful stare made my stomach turn. He still didn't let go of me, but that wild look he gave me stirred me up. My thighs became moist as a a dirty thought of him came into my mind. I tried to rid of it, but the thought grew into an idea. A dangerous idea of him taking me. I couldn't explain why but I wanted him. I hated him with every fiber of his being, yet, in that second, I wanted this man like the air I breathed.

My eyes focused on his thick dark lips. My mouth watered imagining how they would feel on mine during a lingering kiss. My eyes couldn't stray from his muscular figure in his shirt. The shirt wasn't tight on him, yet his muscles made the outfit seem two sizes smaller. Honestly there was something wrong with me. Why was i attracted to him. Why did a single drop of his sweat rolling down his body turn me into goo. My legs trembled as my eyes drifted lower to his crotch. I spied the distinct bugle in his shorts. He was big. I didn't even have to see to know he had a package. His shorts reveled much of his size and the air caught in my throat the moment I spotted his thick snake in his pants.

My eyes returned to his and we both stared at each other. What was coming over me. I hate him yet...

He pressed his lips onto mine and too my breath away. I gasped feeling his tongue on mine and the kiss was unexpected but welcomed. I pushed him away and stood in shock.

"Shit, I'm sorry, I..."

Before he could finish, I jumped into his arms and he caught me, holding my ass our lips crashed into each other once more as we kissed passionately.

"Wait..."

"Stop. Just fucking stop." I snapped. "Just go with it."

"Fine." He growled, carrying me towards the lockers.

I ground my ass over his cock making him hard. He groaned and his finger slipped inside my panties and fingered me, and I moaned. I licked his neck and bit his skin. He growled and he clutched me tighter.

"Fuck me..." I whispered, pushing his shorts down.

He grinned and pushed me against the lockers. He removed my panties and slipped inside me. With me pinned against the wall, he fucked me hard, growling letting out every frustration he had about me. I moaned, closing my eyes, feeling his cock piling through me. My legs crossed around his torso, and I moaned.

"That's all you got?" I grunted, taking his hard cock. "No wonder we can't work together. You can barely fuck right."

"Excuse me?"

"Put me down."

He placed me down and I pushed him onto the bench. I grabbed his hard, slick cock covered in my pussy juices and, jerked him off a bit before sitting on his stiffness.

Placing my hands on his chest, I bounced on his cock wildly, twerking my ass giving him a show.

"This is how you fuck a woman." I moaned, enjoying his warm pulsing cock inside me.

"Yeah?" He grinned, smacking my ass.

"Of course."

"This isn't how your fuck a woman."

"Are you sure? It feels good. "

"You haven't came yet."

"It's coming."

"Nah, I'll make you come. I'll make you drip all over the floor when I'm done with you."

"Prove it."

He smirked and smacked my ass. "Get off. Let me prove it to you."

Chapter 5

I grinned and stroked my hard cock. I loved fucking her. The tension that we had made the sex ten times better.

"Bend over the bench."

She gave me a naughty grin and bent over. I hiked her skirt up to her stomach and slid into her. Fuck me was she tight. Holding her hips, I crashed into her. Grunting like a madman I took her. Every time our bodies collided, she moaned. We were freaks, both taking out our frustrations on each other.

"Yes, yes, yes." She moaned.

"That feel good, baby?"

"Baby?"

"Stop it. Don't ruin this."

"What can I say, I'm a dick." I slapped her ass, and she laughed.

"Yeah, you are." She arched her back, and my cock trembled looking at her perfect heart shaped ass.

"Don't lie, you like it." I groaned powering into her.

"Yeah, I do."

"And I like your uptightness. It's annoying but it's also a turn on."

"You're crazy, but I think we're actually a good team."

"What makes you say that?" I teased her by yanking her head back pulling her ponytail. She moaned and giggled. She gave me a naughty smile before I pushed her flat against the floor and kissed her once more. She moaned as we shared a sloppy erotic kiss.

"You've made me come," she breathed.

"Yeah, it didn't sound like it." I grunted, pinning her to the ground.

"Trust me you did." She uttered.

"No, I didn't. I haven't heard you moan my name. Say it."

"Trevor."

"No, say it louder. Scream it. Let everyone know we're fucking in her." I slapped her ass and gasped.

"Fuck me. Fuck me. FUCK ME TREVOR!" She yelled. Her voice vibrated off the walls as she came once more. I grinned and smacked her ass. Watching as her juicy beige fat jiggle.

"That's a good girl." I bit my lip as I felt my own pleasure grow.

"Where did you want me come."

"On my face."

"Really?"

"Yeah, I like the taste of come."

"Oh, shit, I knew you were a freak." I pulled out of her and Grace fell to her knees opening her mouth as my cock spurted cum all over her face, painting her tan face with my white sperm. When I was through, she grinned at me, licking the tip of my cock, swallowing my seed. It was sexy as hell.

"Fuck, that was hot."

"It sure was."

"Here let me get you a towel."

"Thanks," she grinned with my cum dripping off her face.

I grabbed a towel from the bathroom and handed it to her. She cleaned her face and as she was doing it, I couldn't stop smiling at her.

"What?" She asked.

"Nothing, it's just. I never realized how sexy you are."

"You're pretty sexy too." She grinned, tossing the dirty towel in the bin.

"I'm surprised a man hasn't locked you up." I noted, placing my shorts back on.

"Don't have time for men. I want to win a tennis open." After placing on her panties, she adjusted her skirt and tightened her ponytail.

"I heard that. That's why I'm single."

"Really? For the love of the game, right?"

"Yeah."

"Can I ask you a question?" She asked me.

"Sure."

"Did you want to keep doing this? Tennis can be stressful, but sex, I'd don't know, it relaxed me." She admitted.

"Same. Honestly, we were both uptight out there. Perhaps now we can actually play together. I know your moves now and you know mine."

"Exactly. Let's go and find coach and tell him we want to keep playing."

He nodded and followed me out of the locker room.

Chapter 6

Our coach was surprised that we wanted to work together again. Little did he know that we had worked each others' differences out. During practice we were one. Every ball hit to us was slapped back to the other team. We really played well together and the angry heart pounding sex that we had in the the locker room was the reason why. We played so well that not only did we win the US Open. We won all the other tennis opens and the Olympics too. We were a dominant team not only on the court, but in life too. From that moment in the locker room, our relationship grew. We were not only teammates, but lovers too. Trevor became my husband, we had two kids and lived happily ever after.

Enduring Love
Chapter 1

The moment the Japanese bombed Pearl Harbor I knew my life was going to be different. As a Japanese American college student, I was used to walking through my university's hallways as if I was invisible, but after December 7th, it felt like I was the one who bombed the navy base. Never before did I get such nasty stares from my colleagues. They spat at me, threw stuff at me, called me Jap and other racist names.

I hated it. The worst of all, I was as much as an American as they were. My parents immigrated to the States, and I was born in California. I was raised as an American, I spoke fluent English, went to baseball games, enjoyed swing music, and loved drinking Coke.

Walking back from class, I held my schoolbooks when I heard the usual racist insults.

"Hey Jap!" A man shouted at me.

I ignored him and kept my head up.

"Hey Jap, I'm talking to you!" The white man yelled at me.

I heard his footsteps follow me and my heart raced. Normally they would leave me alone once I walked by, he didn't.

"Leave me alone!" I snapped.

"Or what? You're going to get you jap family to come and bomb me too? Fuck you! Go back to your country Jap."

"I'm American asshole!" I yelled back at you.

He spat in my face and the crowd around us laughed. "You ain't American. You are the furthest thing from it. You're a Jap. You're lower than trash. You are nothing!"

He approached me his eyes narrowed and his fist balled. I didn't know what he was going to do to me as I stumbled backwards in fear.

I tripped and the university students around me all laughed.

"You don't deserve to live..." he growled. "I've already signed up for the Marines and I can't wait to kill every single one of you. I'm might as well start with you first..." he grinned.

"Wait no...." I crawled backwards into two more white men, and they smiled, bringing me to my feet, holding my arms out.

"Keep her steady boys..." the man grinned as he attempted punch me.

I closed my eyes waiting for the strike to come but it never came. Instead, I saw a large muscular African man in front of me. He held the white man's fist and glared at him.

"It ain't right to hit a lady."

"Get your hands off me, nigger."

"No, leave her alone."

"You'd get yours too." He growled attempting to break free from the black man's strong grasp.

"No, I won't. You've done enough. Obliviously your mama ain't teach you right. Perhaps instead of picking on women, you head on into class and learn something."

"How dare you! Fellas!"

The two men who held me, let go and charged towards my defender.

"Watch out!" I yelled, but apparently, he needed no warning. He yanked the man he held on to and tossed him into the group of two others. The three toppled to the ground and the black man held up his fists ready for the fight to come.

The three men, hopped to their feet and challenged the black man, but my savior beat them all with ease. Jabbing left and right, he left all three men bloodied on the floor. I smiled watching him defend me and felt something my chest for the muscular black hero in front of me.

I heard a whistle and the sound of footsteps. Looking down the hall I saw campus police charging towards us.

Without thinking, I grabbed the man's hand and ran away from the crowd with him.

"What the..." he gasped, his eyes opened wide with surprise.

"It's campus police. If they catch us, they throw us both out of the school…" I yelled, running through the halls.

He gave me a small smile and ran beside me. We kept running until we were out of the study hall and onto the campus mall. Once outside, we stopped and caught our breath.

"Thanks for that." I grinned.

"No, thank you. My parents would kill me if they found out I got kicked out of college. They are paying for my schooling."

"Same here." I laughed. "My name is Charlotte Sato."

"Charles Williams." His smile was one in a million

"Nice to meet you, Mr. Williams." I brushed back my curls and held my hand out. Seeing my gesture is smile triple and he shook it with a firm grip.

"Same here, Miss Sato. Well, I ought to be going…"

"Wait…"

He paused and looked deep into my eyes. His stare made me tremble.

"I ugh…" I couldn't find the words at first. How could this gentle giant give me butterflies? "Sorry," I touched my forehead and smiled at him. "Did you want to take a walk with me?"

"I'd love to."

I grinned back at him and followed closely beside him down the path towards the dorm rooms.

"Thank you again for saving me."

"Welcome. I couldn't stand watching them belittle you like that."

"You're not angry at me either?"

"Why? You didn't bomb the harbor. I'm used to people hating someone based on the color of their skin instead of the character in their hearts."

"That's sweet."

He smiled and looked down at his shoes before looking back at me. I couldn't tell, but it appeared he was blushing.

We were silent for a moment before I spoke up. "Does it hurt when they call you nigger?"

"All the time, but it's important to not let them see it bother you. You did right by keeping your head up."

"Thanks. I'm afraid, the insults would only get worse from here. Now that we've declared war against Japan, more and more people would see me less as an American."

"I'm sorry."

"It's okay."

"If you'd want, I can walk with you around campus."

"You'd do that?"

"Yeah, what, is your class schedule like? We can try and meet up somewhere?"

"I have intro to bio at 9 and then English 101 at 10, then calculus at 12."

"I have those same classes."

"Really?! I don't see you in class at all."

"I sit in the back." He replied.

"Ah, okay." I grinned. "Perhaps we can study together. "

"I'd like that."

His warm smile, made my heartbeat twice its pace. I didn't know it then, but that conversation was the start of my new relationship with Charles.

Chapter 2

I couldn't stop crying once I heard the news.

I could see the concern on Charles face when I met him outside his dorm room. We've been meeting in this spot for his past two months. Over that time, he's became my best friend. We hung out together, studied together, ate meals together. He made me laugh and smile. Even when everyone else gave us dirty looks, he kept me in good spirits. It was safe to say Charles meant more to me than any man I had in my life. I was so thankful for him, which is why when I got the news from my parents of a letter that came to our house, I was upset.

His eyes narrowed and his fists clenched ready for a fight.

"Charlotte, what happened?" He asked, brushing a tear from my cheek.

"My parents had called me and told me the government wants to put us in camps."

"Why?"

"Because we are Japanese. They fear that we will revolt against them. So, they think it's safer for us to be in camps."

"They can't do that! It goes against the 14th amendment."

"Apparently they can."

"No, we are going to fight this. I'm going to fight this."

"Charles...you can't fight everything. This law is nationwide. I am to go back home next week so the government can bus us to the new location."

"No...no...no... you can't leave."

"I'm sorry, Charles."

"I'm going to fight this. I'm going..."

I didn't know what drove me on my next actions, but I couldn't stop it. I had to feel his lips on mine. I kissed him and he breathed deeply holding my tightly deepening our kiss. When we pulled away, he stared at me in shock.

"What was that for?"

"I didn't want to leave you without showing you how I truly feel. These last two months have been special. You were there for me when no one else was. You were my friend. I love you."

"Marry me." He replied.

"Charles..."

"Marry me." He repeated.

"But..."

"I can't control what is going to happen in the next week, but I can control right now. I know you love me. I know I love you. That alone is enough for me. I don't want to live in a world without you. The government is taking you away from me, and I can't stand it. Marry me, so at least for a day we have each other."

"I will. Of course I will marry you."

Charles smiled and kissed me once more. We skipped class and drove to the courthouse to get married. Of course, the clerk laughed us. She thought she'd seen it all, but apparently seeing a *nigger and a jap get married tops the cake*, her words not mine.

We didn't let her hate bother us. Nothing was going to stop us. Not even the government. As far as the country and the state of California was concerned, I was Charlotte Williams-Sato and nothing was going to change that.

Chapter 3

After marrying my best friend, Charles took me to the hotel room we had rented. He carried up up the stairs and placed me down to open the door.

Once inside, he kissed me again and led me towards the bed.

"Charlotte?"

"Yes?" I breathed as he peppered my neck with delicate kisses.

"Can I have you?"

"You already do..." I grinned, and he smiled back at me. He lifted me up and placed me on the bed. His large hands slid down my delicate feminine sides, exploring every inch of me as we kissed. As he laid on top of me, I felt his large bulge on my leg.

I'd never had sex before, and he hadn't either. I didn't know what to expect, but from what my mother told me, making love was a magical experience.

My hand clutched his shirt, and I unbuttoned it. Once he was shirtless, my hands slid down his sculpted dark-skinned body. My fingers tingled touching his muscles. I loved the color of our skin mixing together. He was brown, I was beige, and we were both untied by our love.

His lips crashed into mine, and he unzipped my pink dress. I stood up and allowed the dress to drop off my shoulders, exposing myself to him. His yes opened wide seeing me in my bra and underwear. He smiled and whispered, "you are beautiful. I am so happy you are mine."

"As am I, husband."

It felt strange saying those words, but at the same time it felt right.

He held my cheek and planted another kiss on my lips. As we kissed, I felt his hands reach for my bra. He struggled with it and laughed.

"Sorry I..."

"It's okay. Let me." I unhooked my bra, and the moment Charles saw my breasts his eyes opened wide.

"Can I?" He asked.

I nodded and he reached out and grasped my body. His large hands kneaded and massaged my skin and nipples. I groaned and tilted my head back. He then leaned forward and sucked on my erected tips.

I groaned and reached down towards his pants. I unzipped his pants, and he paused kissing my chest to remove his clothes. Seeing his large member made me tremble.

"Are you okay?" He asked.

"Yes, just nervous. You are my first."

"As you are mine, but I'm happy."

"Me too." I grinned.

He kissed me once more, and then removed my underwear. I shivered feeling the cool air brush across my moist opening. Laying there, I felt exposed, but I liked the feeling. I liked the way he looked at me and held me. He was bigger than me and when my slim body wrapped around his muscular frame it just felt right. Seconds later he slipped inside me. It was tight and I groaned from the pain coming over me.

"Are you okay?" He asked

"Yes, it just hurts."

"Did you want to stop?"

"No, keep going. I want this. I want you."

He grinned and cupped my face. Slowly he thrusted, his lips never leaving mine as we made love. The pain soon subsided and there was only pleasure. Closing my eyes, I moaned and finally understood why my mother called this moment magical. I was in heaven, and I didn't want to leave.

Charles held me tightly and groaned, thrusting deeply and sensually. I held his back, and my legs rose slightly allowing him to enter me further. Once again, I moaned from the blooming feeling in my core.

I gasped as the pleasure exploded inside me and I felt a warm gush between my thighs. Charles must have felt it as well as he groaned once more. He body trembled and I felt him squirt inside me. When he was through, he held me tightly.

"I love you." He whispered, cuddling me.

"I love you too. What do you think will happen to me?"

"I don't know, but God help this country if they hurt you. I will lose it if I lose you."

"Really?"

"Yes, I'll be waiting for you. I promise."

"Will you?"

"Doesn't matter if they put you away for months or years, I will wait for you until the end of my days."

"Aww Charles. I love you."

"I love you too Charlotte."

He kissed me once more before, laying beside me. We made love throughout the night. We didn't want to leave the bed as we were both afraid that once we left it we'd never see each other again. Later that week, I left campus and headed back home to take the bus to the concentration camp. Charles with me the entire time until the gates of the camp closed behind me.

Chapter 4

When the gates finally opened, my son, Charles Jr, and I were finally free. Charles looked just like his father, and I couldn't wait for him to meet him. It had been four years since the government imprisoned us and I prayed that Charles kept his promise. As the bus left the station, I stood at the terminal waiting for Charles. I then heard a familiar voice call out and turned to see my husband. He had tears in his eyes as he ran to see me.

"Charlotte!" He screamed. He picked me up and twirled me in the air. After giving me a deep kiss he placed me down and looked at his son.

"Is that my?" He asked swelled with emotion.

I nodded. "Charles Jr, would you like to meet your father?"

"Hi, daddy?" Our son waved.

Charles wept and held his son for the first time. He kissed his forehead and kissed me. "Come on, let's go home."

We all left the station in smiles as we were finally together again. The war may have separated us, but it never broke our love. Through all the hardships we found each other again, living happily ever after.

The Marriage Mix Up

He frowned the first time he saw me. I could see it in his eyes, I wasn't what he expected. He was black, I was white. He had corse dark hair, I had curly red auburn hair. His eyes color was as dark as night like his skin, and mine were as blue as the sky. In this country it was frowned upon that our two skin colors would marry. Yet, there I stood on the porch of his home, in front of my legally wedded husband.

"This isn't right..." he breathed, shaking his head in disbelief.

"No, I think it is. You are Robert Washington, living on the farmhouse property on 123 Green Street of Greenville, Texas?"

"Yes, that's me." He gasped. "And you are, Mary Taylor, from Houston, Texas?"

"Yes, I am."

"And you used the mail order bride service, American Wives for American Husbands?"

"Yes, I did. You wrote to me..." I replied, pulling out the various letters we shared with each other over the last few months.

"How can this be...." He mumbled, looking at the words of affection we shared during the pen pal stage of our relationship. "You ain't black."

"I no but...."

He cut me off before I could answer.

"I was assured that the section of wives I was picking from were of African descendants."

"I am of African decent. I'm one fourth African to be exact."

"But you are white..." he repeated, his eyes couldn't look away from my physical appearance.

"Yes, you made that clear. My skin may be pale, my hair red, and my eyes blue, but my ancestry isn't. I guess, the legality of my heritage allowed us to be married. You see in America although I may look white, in the eyes of law I am still black."

"Oh..."

"Yes, may I come in?" I asked pointing towards the door.

He nodded and allowed me to walk into his large farmhouse home. The living space was vast with several sofas and bookcases. For single man, he lived neatly with barely a speck of dust to be seen on the cherrywood furniture.

"Is it just you here?" I asked, searching the house expecting to see either a maid or children.

"Yes, just me. This house and cattle ranch is all mine. I got five other African families living on my property too. They help with the farm and cows."

I nodded examining his property. His watched me dutifully, and removed his hat, placing it over his chest.

"Miss, I'm sorry, but I just don't understand. How can someone looking like you, want to be married to me? With your pale skin, you could be married to any white man."

"Honestly, I'm just looking for a better life. Yes, I may look white, but as soon as someone finds out about my true heritage, they discard me. In this world, being mixed race like me is difficult to find a husband. I only look this way because my mother, who was half black, was a whore. White men loved to fuck her because they felt like she was exotic. She wanted the best for me, and when a rich patron knocked her up, she managed to get child support from him."

"Oh..."

"Yes, but my mother died a few years back and since then, my biological father wanted nothing to do with me. I've been living on my own since then. Trying to find a man to take care of me. Every black man I meet is afraid to talk to me because they think I'm white, and every white man is disgusted by me because I'm mixed. All I want is a husband and to be loved. That is why I signed up for the mail order service. I want a man to take care of me."

"Why didn't you say anything in our letters?"

"Because I didn't want you to judge me on my physical appearance. I wanted you to fall for me. I wanted you to want me just on the fact that you were searching for a wife."

"Yes, but as my wife, don't you think we would be called out on the street? A black man and white woman together down Main Street isn't going to sit right with a lot of folks. Especially down here in the south. I may be rich and popular with the locals, but I am still black. There's a way in order here."

"No, but it won't matter. In the eyes of the law, we are married. The courthouse approved it. We have the marriage license signed off by the county clerk. They have my family ancestry and know that I'm legally African. Let the law come down on us, in the end they will learn of my African heritage and know that our marriage is valid."

He shook his head. "It's too risky. The last thing I want is to be strung up by some misunderstanding. One look at your red hair hair and blue eyes, the white man will surely hang me from a tree for touching you."

"No, they won't. I promise."

"I may have your word, but I ain't risking my life. I'm sorry, but I'm going to have to contact the mail order bride service. We are going to have to set for a divorce." He began to walk towards the door to leave but I grabbed his hand.

"Wait!"

"No, I'm sorry, Mary, but this ain't gonna work."

"Robert, please don't. I don't want to go back to the service. I know you are a good man. I'm sorry for deceiving you, but I had no other choice. I don't want no other man but you."

"Yes, but our skin color..."

"Is it really just the color of my skin that turns you ill?"

"No. I think your beautiful but..."

"Then what? Why do you run?" I take a step closer to him and hold his hand, peering deep into his eyes. He stood stiff as board, unable to move or speak, watching my every move. "We are married. This piece of paper says so..." I held up the marriage license and show him. He looked at the document and then back at me. "Before you go, shouldn't we explore all aspects of our marriage?"

"Like what?" He murmured.

"Make love to me."

"Mary..."

I kissed him before he could speak another word and his body went rigid. Holding his face, I looked lovingly into his eyes and whispered, "Fuck me, and find out if you still want me. If the sex ain't good, then you are free to contact the service and get a divorce from me, but if you enjoy my pleasure, be my husband. Stay with me. Allow me to be your wife, allow me to have your babies, and fill this large empty house with joy."

He paused and hesitated.

My hand crept down towards his crotch, and I grabbed his cock through his pants. Slowly, I stroked his length and whispered in his ears.

"You can at least say you've fucked a white woman. What do you say? Do you want to see what your black cock looks like slipping in and out of a tight white pussy like mine?"

He stiffened and I knew I had him where I wanted.

He breathed deeply and stared at me.

"Is that a, yes?"

He nodded.

"Good." I kissed him once more and grabbed his hand, leading him towards the bedroom. Once inside, I led him to the bed and we both sat on the edge kissing each other. Slowly, we removed our clothes until we were both naked.

His eyes widened looking at my naked figure. I could tell he was impressed by my feminine curves. He didn't speak a word, but he didn't have to. His eyes said it all as he gazed at me like a goddess.

I climbed on top of his hard black cock and sunk down on his rod. Fuck was I wet. Not to mention it felt great feeling his big black cock stretch me out. We were made for each other.

I made sure to put on a show, moaning and groaning as I sensually rode up and down his long length.

He breathed heavily, watching me pleasure him. His eyes were wide as he palmed my pale flesh. His hands couldn't stay off me as he fondled my ass and breasts. His eyes didn't leave my perky tits as they jiggled with every bounce. A small smile curled on his lips as he kneaded my pale bust with his dark hands.

Leaning forward he sucked my tit. His large tongue swirled around my pink nipple, making the tip hard. He lightly nibbled at it like a newborn making my own pleasure grow.

"How is it?" I muttered.

"Good," he breathed.

"Do you like fucking me?"

"Yes."

"Do you like fucking my white pussy?"

"Yes."

"Do you want to be my husband?"

"Yes..." he muttered.

I grinned, knowing that I had him. He was mine. I was his.

"Then prove it. Fuck me hard. Leave your seed in me. Make me yours forever."

A naughty smile spread across his face as he grabbed me and tossed in the bed. He gained the dominant postion on top and pushed my legs behind my head. He pounded my pussy like madman. He growled like a beast, fucking me hard. I fucking loved the aggression. It was passionate and breathtaking. I moaned, holding his muscular hips begging to him to fuck me faster and harder.

His pace was demonic. He was possessed. I could tell he loved every second of having me. I was different than any other woman he had. Eyes couldn't stray of the beautiful mosaic our two skin colors made. I was white. He was black. In this country we shouldn't be together, yet we were together on a technicality, and we loved every second of it.

He groaned when he finished, and I felt his seed fill me up. When he was through, he gasped and pulled out of me, watching as his cum leaked from my gaping pussy.

I gasped, placing a hand above my sweaty forehead. I grinned and grabbed his chin to kiss him.

"So, can I stay your wife?" I teased.

"Of course..." he replied.

"Good. I am happy to be married to you Robert Washington."

"As I'm I Mary Washington."

Hearing my new last name gave me chills. I laughed and rolled on top of him. I kissed him once more, sealing our new love forever. Although we had different skin colors, our love never faltered. We fought the racism together, as husband and wife, and lived happily ever after.

Don't miss out!

Visit the website below and you can sign up to receive emails whenever Hunter Briggs publishes a new book. There's no charge and no obligation.

https://books2read.com/r/B-A-TGQJB-AIQAF

BOOKS2READ

Connecting independent readers to independent writers.

Did you love *An Erotic Interracial Romance*? Then you should read *An Erotic Interracial Romance Volume 4*[1] by Hunter Briggs!

A collection of five short erotic romance stories. Each story contains a steamy romance between a WWBM couple or a LWBM couple. In this collection you will find five heart racing erotic romances about an a college athlete falling in love with his biggest fan, two best friends falling in love together after making a pact, a BBW wants her BBW to join her black husband in a trouple, a foreign Latina woman marries a black man from the internet, and a busty woman finds romance with a muscular black cop! Each one of these stories, features sexy a Asian woman or white woman along with a hunky handsome black man! This collection is perfect for anyone looking for multiple stories of steamy, passionate love!

---

1. https://books2read.com/u/bPGMgJ

2. https://books2read.com/u/bPGMgJ

Also by Hunter Briggs

An Erotic Interracial Romance
The Kiss
The Recruitment
The Football Trainer
The NIL Deal
Shipwrecked
Falling for My Friend
Seducing My Roommate
My Arranged Marriage
Loving an Older Woman
Taken by a Black Man: The Asian BBW
The African Samurai's Consort
My Filipino Wife
The Ultimatum
The Swimsuit BBW
My Biggest Fan
The Pact
Sharing my Black Husband with my BBW Best Friend
The Badge Chaser
My Green Card Wife
Going for Gold
My Truth
The Marriage Mix Up

On the Beach
Mixed Doubles
Enduring Love

BBC Only
Finding a Baby Daddy
The Milf Next Door
Mrs. Williams
An Easy A
Seeking Young Black Stud
Taken by My Black Slaves
Taken by the Football Team
Cheating on My Wife
Riding My Slave
Coworkers
Betraying My Country
Taken by a Black Man: My Best Friend's Mom
Hidden Pleasures
The African Warlord and his Chinese Consort

Big, Bold, and Beautiful Women
Falling for My Boss
My Best Friend's Hot Brother
The Hot Single Dad Next Door

Black Billionaire Club
Claimed by the Black Billionaire: The Homeless Housewife
Claimed by the Black Billionaire: The Spanish Housewife

Claimed by the Black Billionaire: The Chinese and Indian Diplomats
Claimed by the Black Billionaire: The Shoplifting Housewife
Claimed by the Black Billionaire: The Bartender
Claimed by the Black Billionaire: The Filipino Milf

Bundles
Cougars Want Black Meat
Big, Bold and Beautiful Women Bundle 1
Only BBC
An Erotic Interracial Romance: Volume 1
I Like it Black: Raw and Uncensored
Paranormal, Strange and Sci-Fi Erotica: Volume 1
An Erotic Interracial Romance: Volume 2
An Erotic Interracial Romance: Volume 3
Hot & Steamy Erotic Shorts Collection
An Erotic Interracial Romance Volume 4
An Erotic Interracial Romance

Hot & Steamy Erotic Shorts
Golden Wok
My Last Night before Deployment
I Think My Neighbor is a Hooker
The Red Room Inn
Danny's Mom

Paranormal, Strange and Sci-fi Erotica
Taken by the Redneck Killer
The Pill

The Werewolf and Sexy Babe

Standalone
The Mechanic
Hot For Teacher
Yes, Professor
Making My Son A Man
Tattle Tale
Claimed by the Black Billionaire: Volume 1
Getting Out of a Ticket
Cheating with My Black Neighbor
Basting My Girlfriend's Mom
Online Hookup: A Curvy WWBM Spicy Romance

About the Author

Hunter Briggs is an interracial romance erotica author. He loves writing out of the box stories, that at are different from the rest. If you like reading about tall, dark and handsome alphas and beautiful, thick thighed women, then Hunter Briggs is the author for you. If he's not writing hot, burn a hole in your panties erotica, Hunter Briggs is lazily watching TV because he has no other cool hobbies like other authors. Hunter Briggs is a loving husband and father and while he owns no dogs, he has always wished for a furry friend. He enjoys anything that can raise his blood pressure including, spicy buffalo wings, onion rings and ice-cold beer.

Follow me on Twitter: @Briggs_Romance